Stalling

Alan Katz

Illustrated by

Elwood H. Smith

Margaret K. McElderry Books

New York London Toronto Sydney

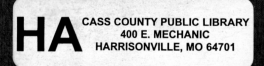

The following images were photographed by the illustrator, Elwood H. Smith, and composed digitally by Maggie Pickard: yardstick (pp. 10–11); dominoes (pp. 11, 36); vintage cymbal-playing chimp (pp. 13, 36); rag mops (p. 15); chimes (pp. 16, 36); magnifying glass (pp. 17, 32–33); electric mixer (p. 17); telephone (p. 18); baseball (pp. 19, 36); toenail clippers (p. 22); pencil (p. 26); bicycle pump and hose (p. 27); envelope (p. 31). The following images were composed digitally by Maggie Pickard: fan (pp. 16, 36); numeral cue balls (pp. 32, 36–37). The glitter paint swipe (p. 27) was created courtesy of Obsidian Dawn, www.obsidiandawn.com. The camel image (pp. 31, 36) is used with permission of the photographer, Riyas Hamza, and the source, StockXchng.

MARGARET K. McELDERRY BOOKS

An imprint of Simon & Schuster Children's Publishing Division

1230 Avenue of the Americas, New York, New York 10020

Text copyright © 2010 by Alan Katz

Illustrations copyright © 2010 by Elwood H. Smith

MARGARET K. McELDERRY BOOKS is a trademark of Simon & Schuster, Inc.

For information about special discounts for bulk purchases, please contact Simon & Schuster Special Sales at 1-866-506-1949 or business@simonandschuster.com.

The Simon & Schuster Speakers Bureau can bring authors to your live event. For more information or to book an event, contact the Simon & Schuster Speakers Bureau at 1-866-248-3049 or visit our website at www.simonspeakers.com.

Book edited by Emma D. Dryden

Book designed by Debra Sfetsios

The text for this book is set in Tempus ITC Std.

The illustrations for this book are rendered in India ink and watercolor (with added textures) and assembled in Photoshop.

Manufactured in China

0310 SCP

10 9 8 7 6 5 4 3 2 1

Library of Congress Cataloging-in-Publication Data

Katz, Alan.

Stalling / Alan Katz ; illustrated by Elwood H. Smith. — 1st ed.

p. cm.

Summary: An energetic young boy has many things to do before he is ready to go to bed.

ISBN 978-1-4169-5567-2

[1. Stories in rhyme. 2. Play—Fiction. 3. Bedtime—Fiction.] I. Smith, Elwood H., 1941– ill. II. Title.

PZ8.3.K1275St 2009

[E]—dc22

2007047454

To Emma, for at least
4,167 reasons —A. K.

To my wife, Maggie,
for her love, support,
and creative input
—E. H. S.

"You've got to go to sleep," Mom said.
"Come on, we'll read to you."

"Not time for counting sheep," Dan said.

"First I got stuff to do!"

And he was off!
"I gotta . . . .

use all my pillows to trap armadillos!

Visit the Nile,
tame a crocodile!

See if my height
is more than last night!

Dominoes!
Climb Mount Clothes!
Cross the room on tippy-toes!

Wheeeeeeeeeeeeeeeeeee!

Then . . .

hallway soccer!

Rock the rocker!

Dance real funky with my monkey!

Act like a swami!   Do origami!

Munch on some noodles!
Do a few doodles!

Use mops as oars!

Hide stuff
in drawers!

Make paper fans!

Recycle cans!

Ring a chime!

Solve a crime!

Mix leftovers 'til they're slime!

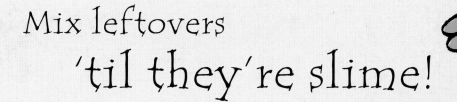

High-five the lizard!

Confetti blizzard!

Train a flea!

Watch TV!

Part my hair . . .

and the Red Sea!

Plus I gotta . . .

wet my towel, say

"I washed!" . . . then howl!

ARROOOOO

Creep like slow snails!
Clip my toenails!

Wrap my tummy
like a mummy!

Yeeeeeeee . . . ha!
Catch a pass,
score a touchdown . . .

but don't knock

the big den hutch down!

Scale a sequoia,
if it won't annoy ya!

Writing! **Knighting!**

Knight

Kung fu fighting!

Then it's time to . . .

inflate a critter!

Paint
with
glitter!

Hunt
for tyrannosaurus!

Lead the fish in chorus!

Mathematics!

Acrobatics!

Fight the fight at Appomattox!

Greetings from MILWAUKEE Wisconsin

Walkie-talkie
with Milwaukee!

A
B

Stack some blocks!

Smell my socks!

Write to Aunt Clara!

Aunt Clara
123 4th St.
Claraville, MI

Brave
the Sahara!

Multiply! Magnify!

Do some tricks that mystify!

Change pajamas, to the ones with the llamas!

Get a crank and crank it!

Hide under a blanket!

Yaaaaaaawn . . . .

I'm finally ready for bed," said Dan.

But his folks didn't hear the news.

'Cause while the kid took time to stall,
they both lay down to snooze.

Yes, kids can outlast parents—
no matter where,
no matter when.

So Dan tucked Mom and Dad in tight,

and went stalling

once again!

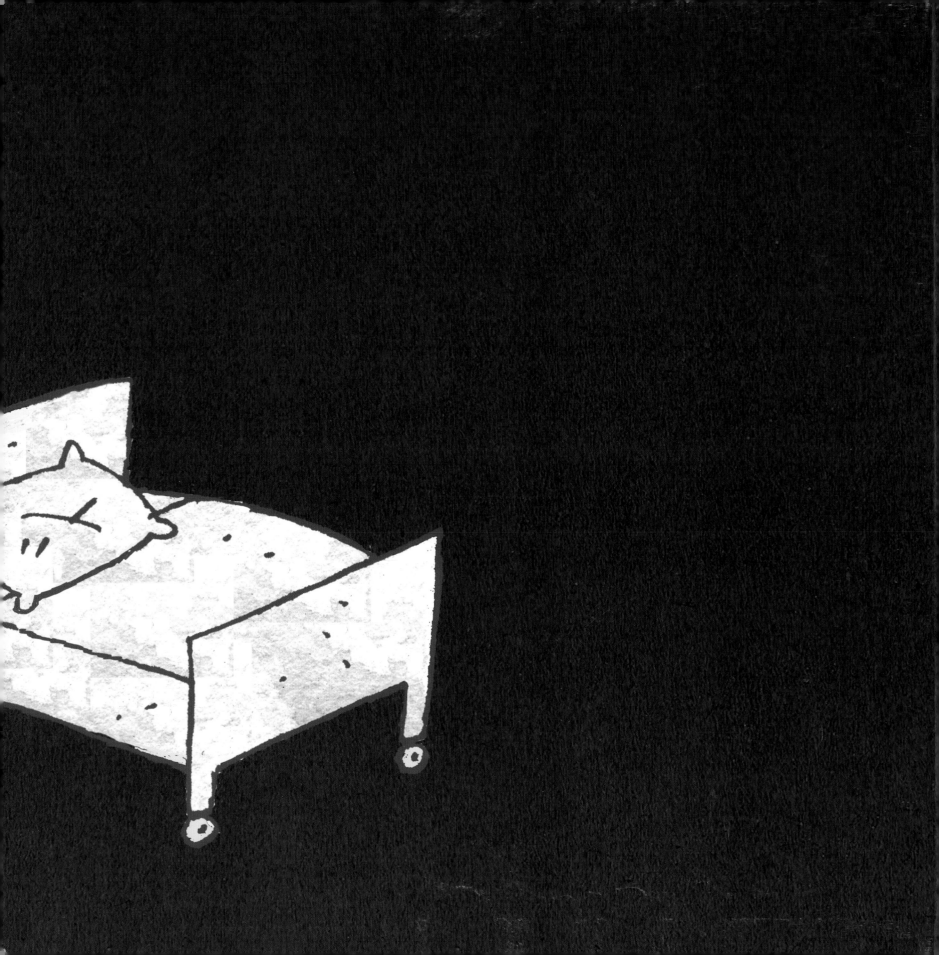